After a career in film and television as a makeup artist, Kate retrained to become a Montessori teacher after the birth of her second son. She currently works as a teaching assistant and runs her own bridal makeup and hair business.

Meryl the Sheep

Kate Bower

AUSTIN MACAULEY PUBLISHERS™
LONDON • CAMBRIDGE • NEW YORK • SHARJAH

Copyright © Kate Bower (2021)

A CIP catalogue record for this title is available from the British Library.

ISBN 9781398428133 (Paperback)
ISBN 9781398428140 (ePub e-book)

www.austinmacauley.com

First Published (2021)
Austin Macauley Publishers Ltd
25 Canada Square
Canary Wharf
London
E14 5LQ

To Kate and Meryl Sheep

Kate Bower

Meryl the Sheep

Thanks to my amazing parents for their constant love, support and encouragement. Also to Les, Josh and Dan for the love and laughter.

Down on the farm the sheep were all grazing,
All except one who was just stood there gazing.
Up into the sky, her head full of dreams,
Lost in her thoughts, ambitions and schemes.

Ever since she was a lamb,
Meryl loved doing am-dram
Her passion was drama,
To play a queen, nurse or farmer.

She was different, not the same,
All she wanted was to entertain.
To sing rather than bleat,
To dance rather than sleep.

So unimpressed were the flock
They would just mock:

"Your job is a sheep,
That's all that you are.
Your job is to follow,
Your job is to go baaaa!"

But Meryl was undeterred
Her passion was stirred.
She would prove them all wrong
She'd be brave, she'd be strong.

Her dreams she would follow,
She wouldn't sit there and wallow.
She would make them all see
What a great actress she could be!

She would put on a show,
Do Shakespeare, sing songs of Manilow,
Dance just like on Strictly,
Do scenes from Agatha Christie.

But the sheep carried on eating
Whilst at the same time bleating:

"Your job is to be a sheep,
Stop being a fool,
Your job is to eat grass,
Your job is to make wool."

Meryl paid no attention.
How dare they even question
Her ability to perform.
Who were they to bring scorn?

So with all the courage she could muster,
She tried not to fluster.
She took to the boards
Awaiting the applause .

But instead all the sheep
Were getting ready to sleep,
More interested in slumber
Than Meryl's dramatic number.

They all shook heads and tutted,
Grumbled and muttered:

"Your job is a sheep,
This has to stop, has to cease!
Your job is to eat grass
And grow a woolly fleece."

"You are only a sheep,
Who do you think you are?
You are Meryl the sheep,
You are no movie star!"

Meryl's little heart was broken
At what the flock had just spoken.
Why hadn't she seen
What a fool she had been?

Too embarrassed to stay,
She left right away,
Her dreams all in shatters,
Her hopes torn to tatters.

All this time patiently waiting
The fox sat contemplating,
Devising a way
To best capture his prey.

As the sheep went to bed,
They quietly said:

"Our job as a sheep
Is to be counted and be shorn,
Meryl has always been differer
Since the day she was born."

Fox saw his chance
And slowly did advance.
Carefully he crept
Up to the flock as they slept.

Skilfully and gently
As the sleep snored contently,
He stepped over the ram
And ran off with a lamb!

The lamb started bleating,
Its tiny heart beating!
The flock were distraught
That their lamb had been caught!

They shouted and cried,
And ran around terrified.

"We are sheep, it's not our job
To be daring or brave.
What will we do?
Our lamb must be saved."

Fox carried on running,
So pleased with his cunning.
But with his den just in sight,
He stopped, frozen with fright!

For there stood before him
A monster so grim,
Its blood-red eyes staring
And huge nostrils flaring!

From its filthy body rose steam
And a smell so obscene.
Swaying and moaning,
It started approaching.

·x's legs started quaking,
s body trembling and shaking.

> "I'm a fox," he said timidly,
> "I mean you no harm.
> It's my job to catch sheep
> Here on this farm."
>
> The monster momentarily paused,
> Raised its razor-sharp claws,
> Pressed its nose to Fox's cheek
> And let out a blood-curdling shriek!

Fox went as white as a sheet,
Dropped the lamb at its feet.
And in an instant he fled
And became a vegetarian instead.

The sheep were delighted,
They were now all reunited.
The fox was defeated.
"We are safe," they all bleated.

But the sheep stopped their cheering
For the monster was nearing!

"We are sheep," they all whimpered,
"Please don't do us any harm,
Our job is to live quietly
Here on this farm."

The monster stroked its chin,
Then it began giggling.
The sheep were confused,
Why was this monster
so amused?

To their great surprise,
They discovered it was Meryl in disguise!
The monster was a fake!
Its claws were just rakes.

Having seen the lamb in such peril,
Without hesitation Meryl
Had leapt into the compost heap
And become the 'monster sheep'.

The sheep cheered and applauded,
Meryl's bravery rewarded.

"Your job is an actress,
How wrong we all are.
You have made us all see
You are our own superstar."

Now by sheer coincidence
Stood watching by the fence
Was a newspaper reporter
Out on a walk with his daughter.

He took pictures and interviews
With Meryl and the ewes,
And the story became so huge
She became a sensation on EweTube.

Meryl's dream had come true,
More adventures she would pursue.
Her heart was fit to burst,
But she needed to say something first.

"Just like you, I am a sheep
And of that I am proud.
But it's okay to be different,
To not follow the crowd."

We all have our talents,
Our weaknesses and strengths.
We just need support as
It may take many attempts."

"But what matters the most
Is how we act as a friend.
We must be kind and be tolerant,
Be careful to not offend."

So offer encouragement,
Be polite but don't pretend.
Because there is nothing more important
Than being a true friend."

Meryl the Sheep dreams of being an actress. She loves nothing better than to sing, dance and entertain. But the other sheep think she should stop being so silly and just be one of the flock. Will Meryl be able to follow her dreams?